For Abi
(the other author of this book)
with much love
M.L.

For Peter and Simone
Pippa, Rob and Mia
A.R.

ORCHARD BOOKS
338 Euston Road, London, NW1 3BH
Orchard Books Australia
Hachette Children's Books
Level 17/205 Kent Street, Sydney, NSW 2000
ISBN 1 84362 868 6
First published in Great Britain in 2006
Text © Michael Lawrence 2006
Illustrations © Arthur Robins 2006
The right of Michael Lawrence to be identified as the author
and of Arthur Robins to be identified as the illustrator of
this work has been asserted by them in accordance with
the Copyright, Designs and Patents Act, 1988.
Designed by David Mackintosh
1 3 5 7 9 10 8 6 4 2
Printed in China

BABY
CHRISTMAS

Michael Lawrence

Illustrated by
Arthur Robins

ORCHARD BOOKS

I T WAS Christmas Eve, and there were lots of presents to deliver down lots of chimneys. But when Father Christmas put on his Christmas suit, Baby Christmas began to cry.

'Oh dear,' said Mother Christmas.

'Oh dear, oh dear, oh deary-me. What can we do to cheer you up?'

To keep Baby Christmas amused,
Mother Christmas dressed him up in
his Baby Christmas suit and sat him
in his Baby Christmas sleigh.
She even gave him a sack of toys
to pretend to deliver.

'There! Now
you're just like
Father!'

But then . . .

'My mince pies!'
Mother Christmas cried.
And away she went to rescue them
before they burnt to
a frizzle,

a frazzle,

a fruppety-froo.

While Mother Christmas was gone another nose began to twitch.

'Nun-nun-nun-nooooooose!'

said Baby Christmas.

Rudolf Junior's nose had never glowed before, but he knew what it meant.

It meant that he was old enough to fly!

'Ho-ho,'

said Baby Christmas.

'Wa-heee,' said he,

as out they flew into

the dark and frosty night.

Father Christmas was just about to set off on his rounds when
Mother Christmas missed her little one.

Mother and Father Christmas searched high and low and low and high for their little lost lad.

Where could he be?

Where could he **be**?

Where **could** he be?

And where was Baby Christmas?

Why, flying
round the
world with
Rudolf
Junior!

Lights
twinkled and winked
and winkled
and twinked
from
one end
of the world
to the
other.

'Ooo,' said Baby Christmas.

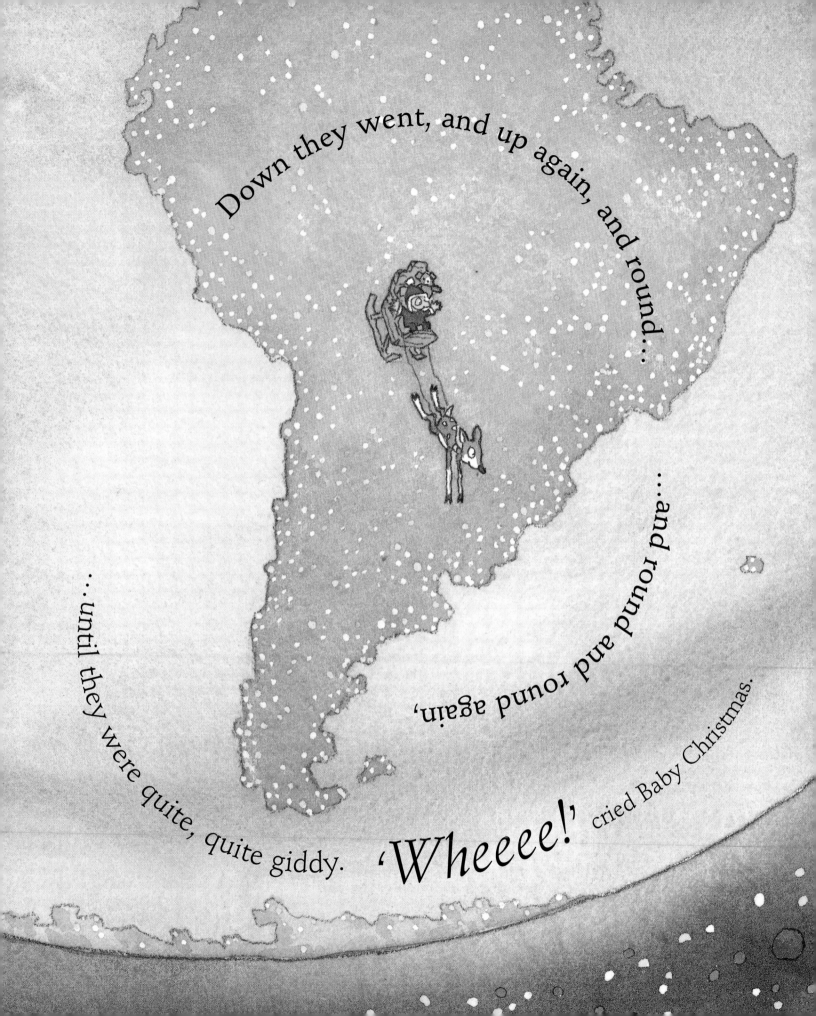

Down they went, and up again, and round....

...and round and round and round again,

'*Wheeee!*' cried Baby Christmas.

...until they were quite, quite giddy.

Rudolf Junior landed on a roof. But his hooves **slipped** and *slithered* and **skidded** and *skaddled,* and...

...into the chimney went Baby Christmas!

Down through the tumbly dark, he fell.

Down and down and down

and down

until...

'Wup!' said Baby Christmas, kerplunking in the hearth.

Mother and
Father Christmas had
searched and searched and
searched for Baby Christmas.

'I want my
bay-hay-hay-
haaay-bee!'

Mother Christmas wailed.

Father Christmas patted her hand.

'Don't fret, Mother.
We'll find him. He'll be
out delivering pressies,
you mark my word.
Right chip off the
old block, that lad.'

In the house, far below, Baby Christmas stared at the big bright tree,

with its lights…

…and tinsel

…and silver bells.

Then he remembered what Father did.

'Yappy Kissmus,' said Baby Christmas.

Baby Christmas looked
out of the window.

The snow was
so thick out there.

Baby Christmas loved the snow!

Suddenly Rudolf Senior
spied a small red glow,
far, far below.

He'd know that nose
anywhere!

Mother and Father
Christmas ran round
and round the garden,
as flustered as custard,
as puffed as pastry.

No sign of Baby Christmas!

But now they saw him!
And what a fuss they made
of him. They picked him
up and hugged him tight,
and smothered him with
Christmas kisses.

But Father had to get on.
It was the busiest night of
the year.
　　　　　All those presents
to deliver, and he hadn't
even started!

Up,
　　they climbed,
　　　　and up
　and up
　　and up,
　　　into the
　　　dark and
　　　　frosty sky.

But as they were nearing home,

Rudolf Junior sneezed.

Aaa–
aaaa–
choooo!

And when he sneezed he lost his balance.

And when he lost his balance...

...his bright red nose took him in another direction entirely.

'Oh no!' cried Mother Christmas. 'Not again!'

After the little sleigh went
Mother and Father Christmas.
And as they went, a single
sound rang out in the dark
and frosty night.

A bubbly little sound.

A very Christmassy little sound.

A tinselly little sound.

Baby Christmas laughing!

Library Services for Schools